海豚双语童书经典回放

图书在版编目（CIP）数据

昆虫会议前的风波 : 汉英对照 / 陶虹改编. -- 北
京 : 海豚出版社, 2015.3
（海豚双语童书经典回放）
ISBN 978-7-5110-1346-0

Ⅰ.①昆… Ⅱ.①陶… Ⅲ.①儿童文学—图画故事—
中国—当代 Ⅳ.①I287.8

中国版本图书馆CIP数据核字(2015)第035178号

书　　名：**海豚双语童书经典回放·昆虫会议前的风波**
作　　者：**陶　虹**

总发行人：**俞晓群**

责任编辑：李忠孝　陈三霞　李宏声
责任印制：王瑞松
出　　版：海豚出版社有限责任公司
网　　址：http://www.dolphin-books.com.cn
地　　址：北京市西城区百万庄大街24号
邮　　编：100037
电　　话：010-68997480（销售）　010-68998879（总编室）
传　　真：010-68998879
印　　刷：北京捷迅佳彩印刷有限公司
经　　销：新华书店及网络书店
开　　本：16开（710毫米×960毫米）
印　　张：1.25　字　数：5千
印　　数：5000
版　　次：2015年3月第1版　2015年3月第1次印刷
标准书号：ISBN 978-7-5110-1346-0
定　　价：17.00元

The insects decided to have an insect convention to judge who was a beneficial insect and who was a harmful insect.

昆虫们决定召开一次昆虫大会来评判谁是益虫，谁是害虫。

One day in early autumn the
insect convention began. **The**
bee was executive chairman.

早秋的一天，昆虫大会开始了。蜜蜂是执行主席。

Mantis and dragonfly were in charge of the examination committee.

螳螂和蜻蜓负责审查委员会。

Ladybug and little gold bee were maintaining order outside the meeting hall.

七星瓢虫和小金蜂在会议厅外维持秩序。

Some insects were rubbing their wings together to make a happy, rhythmic song. This was the convention's marching song.

一些昆虫一起扇动着翅膀，制造出快乐、有节奏的歌曲。这是大会的进行曲。

Other insects showed their invitations so they could enter the meeting hall.

其他昆虫拿出邀请函，以便他们能够进入会议厅。

Spider hurried to the meeting shouting: "Sorry, I'm late."

蜘蛛匆忙地来到会场，喊道："对不起，我迟到了。"

Ladybug and little gold bee stopped the spider: "You can't join the meeting without an invitation."

七星瓢虫和小金蜂拦住蜘蛛说："你们没有邀请函，不能参加会议。"

Spider became angry: "You're all wrong. Everyone knows I'm the best at eating harmful insects!"

蜘蛛很生气："你们都错了，每个人都知道我吃害虫是最棒的！"

"Admission by invitation only." lady-bug still refused to let spider enter.

"凭请柬入场！"七星瓢虫仍然拒绝蜘蛛入场。

Spider shouted: "You are really the lim-it!"

蜘蛛喊道：“你真是障碍！”

Snail and earthworm came rolling along, but ladybug and little gold bee stopped them too.

蜗牛和蚯蚓也慢慢爬过来了，但七星瓢虫和小金蜂也阻挡了他们。

Spider became even angrier: "Let's ask the examination committee!"

蜘蛛更生气了:"让我问一下检查委员会!"

"Why didn't I get an invitation? Why I am not insect?" spider fired a hundred questions at mantis and dragonfly.

"为什么我没有收到邀请？"蜘蛛向螳螂和蜻蜓连连发问。

Mantis patiently explained: "The International Insect Committee has set up a standard. Insects have three pairs of jointed legs. But, you have four pairs of jointed legs. You are an arthropod not an insect."

螳螂有耐心地解释："国际昆虫委员会设立了标准，昆虫有三对有关节的腿。你是节肢动物，不是昆虫。"

"But, aren't we insects?"
snail and earthworm eager-
ly asked.

"但是，我们也不是昆虫吗？"蜗牛和蚯蚓急切地问道。

Mantis answered: "Snail, you are a mollusc and earthworm you are an annelid."

螳螂说："蜗牛，你是软体动物；蚯蚓，你是环节动物。"

After hearing that, spider, earthworm and snail became silent and then went away sulking. The brouhaha was over and the insect convention began.

听到这些，蜘蛛、蚯蚓和蜗牛沉默了，生着闷气走开了。喧闹结束了，昆虫大会开始了。